The Legend of the FOG

Published by Inhabit Media Inc.
www.inhabitmedia.com

Inhabit Media Inc. (Iqaluit), P.O. Box 11125, Iqaluit, Nunavut, X0A 1H0
(Toronto), 146A Orchard View Blvd., Toronto, Ontario, M4R 1C3

Library and Archives Canada Cataloguing in Publication

Mikkigak, Qaunak
The legend of the fog / by Qaunaq Mikkigak & Joanne
Schwartz ; illustrated by Danny Christopher.

ISBN 978-1-926569-45-1

I. Christopher, Danny II. Schwartz,
Joanne (Joanne F), 1960- III. Title.

PS8626.I4183L43 2011 jC813'.6 C2011-905459-0

We acknowledge the support of the Canada Council for the Arts for our
publishing program.

Printed by MCRL Overseas Printing Inc. in ShenZhen, China.
October 2011 #4236106

The Legend of the FOG

by Qaunaq Mikkigak & Joanne Schwartz
Illustrated by Danny Christopher

INHABIT
MEDIA

Well then, I'll tell you the story of a man named Quannguaviniq. His name means one-who-pretends-to-be-frozen because that is just what he had to do one day, long ago. It had been a long, hard winter. Men had gone out hunting and never returned. Strange noises had haunted the nights. Evil spirits seemed to be lurking about. Quannguaviniq had felt uneasy throughout the cold, dark season.

So, when spring finally arrived, Quannguaviniq decided to leave camp and take a walk. He walked along, feeling the crisp air on his face. The snow was almost gone and the earth was hard and brown under his feet. The tundra spread out before him as far as the eye could see. And beyond that, a row of low hills lined the horizon. The cry of a raven pierced the silence. Then it was quiet again.

Suddenly, in the distance, Quannguaviniq could see a man moving swiftly across the tundra, heading right in his direction. The man was enormous and his thundering footsteps made the ground tremble. Even from far away, Quannguaviniq knew it was a tuurngaq, one of the evil spirits he feared. He knew that the tuurngaq would kill him, so thinking quickly, he decided that the only thing to do was to pretend to be dead already. He lay down on the ground, clenched his body as if he were frozen, closed his eyes, and waited.

Soon enough, the tuurngaq came upon Quannguaviniq. Here was just what he wanted. The tuurngaq gave no thought to what might have happened to this man. He only knew he was happy to have found a human to take home and cook for dinner. The man looked dead, but just to make sure, the tuurngaq poked and prodded at Quannguaviniq and indeed found him stiff to the touch. Having brought a carrying sling for just this purpose, the tuurngaq wrapped up the body. After much effort, he finally swung the bundle onto his back and tramped off.

Quannguaviniq bounced along in the sling. He was determined
to make the journey as difficult as possible for the tuurngaq.
Dangling toward the ground, he grabbed every twig and plant
along the way, causing endless snags and delays. The tuurngaq
had to constantly stop to untangle the sling. Then Quannguaviniq
made himself as heavy as he could. The tuurngaq had to walk
slower and slower, constantly adjusting the sling to ease the
burden. The tuurngaq became increasingly cranky and tired.

Finally, the tuurngaq arrived at his dwelling. His wife and son, evil spirits themselves, were waiting for him, greedily licking their lips when they saw the food. He threw the sling down on the ground, grunting and groaning after his difficult journey.

"Wife, tend to the cooking fire," the tuurngaq barked.

He then unwrapped Quannguaviniq, pushed him into the dwelling, and left him standing upright against the wall.

"Son, tell me when the body has thawed out," he yelled.

And with that, he went out to sharpen his axe.

Quannguaviniq could hear the sound of the axe being sharpened. With only the tuurngaq's son in the dwelling, he decided to open his eyes and look around.

When the tuurngaq's son saw this, he jumped up in surprise and yelled to his father, "Father, the food has opened its eyes!"

The tuurngaq yelled back, "It's only thawing!"

The boy looked back at the food and its eyes were closed.

Maybe he had been imagining things. A little while later, though, Quannguaviniq opened his eyes to look around again.

Frightened once more, the son yelled to his father, "Father, the food has opened its eyes!"

The tuurngaq, even more impatient, yelled louder, "It's only thawing!"

Now, the tuurngaq was very tired from his exhausting day. When the axe was sharpened, he came back inside the dwelling and threw it down on the floor. Quannguaviniq did not move a muscle. The tuurngaq looked him over, poking and prodding him. Satisfied that he was thawing nicely, the tuurngaq went to sleep, dreaming of the tasty dinner he would have when he woke up. His son, tired of watching the body thaw out, went to sleep too.

lunged toward the axe and, in one fell swoop, beheaded the evil spirit. The lazy son slept on.

Quannguaviniq dashed outside. As he passed the tuurngaq's wife, he shoved her onto her cooking fire. But this was not enough to stop the wife of a tuurngaq. She jumped up in anger, yelling "aiiiii," brushed the fire off her parka, and without even looking in on her husband and son, started out after the food.

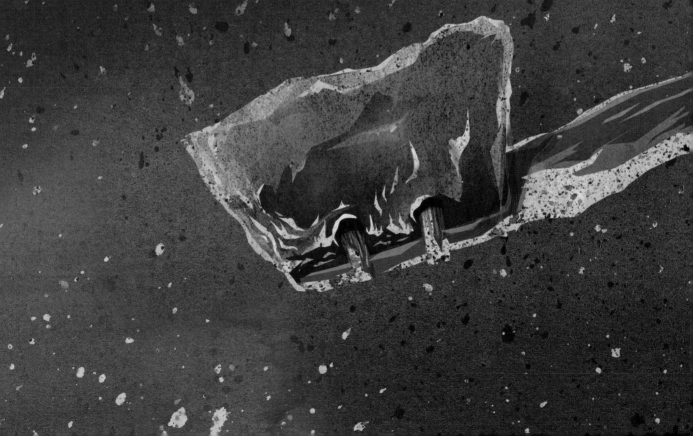

Quannguaviniq ran, and the tuurngaq's wife ran after him. He ran faster, and the tuurngaq's wife ran faster too. Each time he looked back, the tuurngaq's wife was a little closer.

Quannguaviniq was growing tired. He was breathing heavily from running so hard. When he couldn't run anymore, he stopped and crouched down. With his finger he traced a line along the ground, and where he traced the line, a river began to flow. The river became wide and raging. Quannguaviniq stood on one bank of the river, the raging water lapping at his feet. He looked across the water. The tuurngaq's wife had just reached the other side. She stood on the bank shaking her fist.

"How did you cross the river?" she demanded to know.

Quannguaviniq pretended he couldn't hear.

The tuurngaq's wife yelled louder, "How did you cross the river?"

This time Quannguaviniq cupped his hands around his mouth so he could be heard over the raging water. "I drank the river to cross it."

The tuurngaq's wife stepped into the deep water and started drinking. Gulping quickly, she drank and drank. Still not able to cross the river, she drank some more. Finally, so full she could hardly move, she drank even more. And when she couldn't drink another drop, she drank again.

And with that last drop, she burst. Steam rose from her body, swirling into a heavy mist, and then, for the very first time, a thick fog settled over the land.

Quannguaviniq stood in the thick fog. Somewhere in the distance a raven cawed. Slowly, slowly, he made his way home.

Taima.

Afterword

The legend of how fog came to exist can be found in different versions throughout the Canadian Arctic. If you encounter the other versions, you will notice slight variations. The monster, a tuurngaq in this version, could be a giant, a large-bellied ogre, or even a family of grizzly bears that have assumed human form. Occasionally, this legend is found as part of the larger story of Kiviuq, the great Inuit adventurer. Though several details may vary, the legend always tells of a man who uses his wits to outsmart a dangerous adversary. And in the end, due to its own arrogance, the monster is fooled into drinking more water than its body can possibly hold. It then explodes, releasing the first fog into the world.

For many who grew up in the North, childhood was filled with many fantastic myths and legends. But with so many distractions in the world today, the important cultural practice of storytelling has declined. We feel that books of this kind will help ensure that these important pieces of oral history are available for future generations.

If you enjoyed this legend, we encourage you to explore the rich storytelling tradition of Nunavut.

Louise Flaherty and **Neil Christopher**

Contributors

Qaunaq Mikkigak is an elder, artist, and throat singer from Cape Dorset, Nunavut. She was born in 1932 in the Cape Dorset area and grew up on the land in a traditional Inuit community. She was featured in the books *Inuit Women Artists: Voices from Cape Dorset* and *Cape Dorset Sculpture*. She is well known locally for her storytelling, and her throat singing has been featured on several recordings.

Joanne Schwartz was born in Cape Breton, Nova Scotia. She has been a children's librarian in Toronto for over twenty years. Joanne writes reviews and articles for *Canadian Children's Book News* and other publications. Her first picture book *Our Corner Grocery Store* was published in 2009, followed by *City Alphabet* and *City Numbers*. Joanne lives in Toronto with her two daughters. *Our Corner Grocery Store* was nominated for the 2010 Marilyn Baillie Picture Book Award.

Danny Christopher is an illustrator who travels throughout the Canadian Arctic as an instructor for Nunavut Arctic College. Danny lives in Toronto, where he spends much of his time painting and chasing after his two young children.

Iqaluit · Toronto
www.inhabitmedia.com